Olive
the Octopus

Written by Catherine Veitch
Illustrated by Elissambura

In a forest of seaweed
called **giant kelp**, which
grows as tall as trees do
on land, live many animals.

There are spotty fish,
and spiny lobsters...
and an octopus called **Olive**.

One day, **Olive** noticed there was less seaweed around her favourite hidey hole. Olive loved **mysteries**, so she decided to find out who was eating the **seaweed**.

That evening Olive swam into a part of the kelp forest she hadn't visited in some time.

There was less seaweed here, too. Some of the animals had **gone** as well.

Oh no!

"This was my favourite hunting spot."

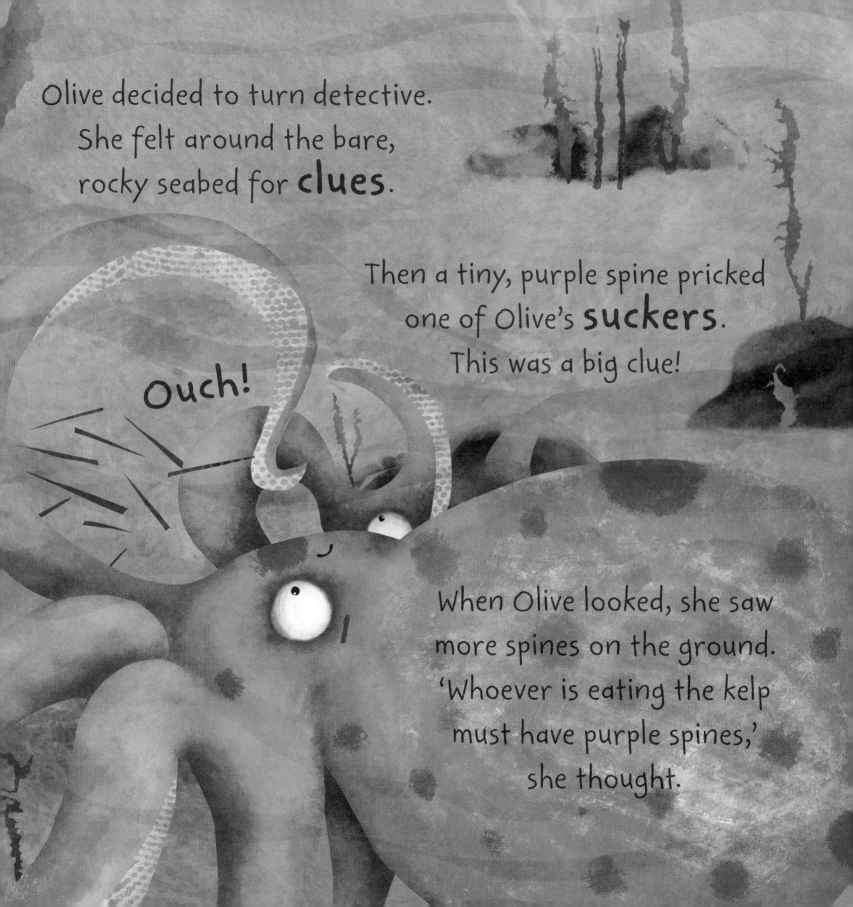

Olive decided to turn detective.
She felt around the bare,
rocky seabed for **clues**.

Then a tiny, purple spine pricked
one of Olive's **suckers**.
This was a big clue!

Ouch!

When Olive looked, she saw
more spines on the ground.
'Whoever is eating the kelp
must have purple spines,'
she thought.

So Olive swam to a part of the forest where lots of **kelp** still grew.

"I will **hide** in this coral and look for an animal with purple spines," she said.

Olive was good at **blending** in with her surroundings. She quickly turned the same colour as the **coral**.

Tee hee!

Olive giggled. "Whoever is eating the seaweed is no match for me!"

Olive kept very quiet as
Bo the **bat ray** swam
past. He did not spot Olive.
Olive looked at Bo closely.

Did he have any
purple spines?

Bo did not. That meant he couldn't be the one eating the seaweed. He was looking for tasty **worms** – not kelp.

Olive did not want to disturb Bo. She stayed **hidden** until he had gone.

The next night, Olive went to another part of the forest where there was still lots of kelp.

There in the rock, she found the **perfect place** to hide.

Olive was good at getting into **small spaces**. She folded up her bendy body and...

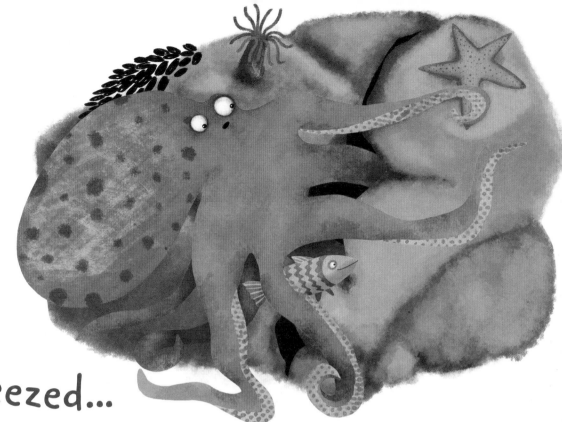

squeeeeeezed...

...into a **teeny, tiny** gap in the rock.

Hush! Olive could hear someone coming.

It was Laynie the **lobster**, scuttling as fast as her legs would carry her.

Rustle!

Scuttle!

Olive looked at Laynie. She had **no purple spines** – so she wasn't eating the kelp.

Then Olive saw who was chasing Laynie. It was Sven, the **giant sea bass**.

Yikes!

Olive stayed hidden – she was scared of Sven. He had **no purple spines** either, so he wasn't eating the kelp.

Olive was not giving up.
On the third night she
went out again.

She was looking hard for another
hiding place, and at first she did not
see some curious **sea lions**
sneaking up on her.

"Argh!" screamed Olive, as a sea lion bumped into her. Olive did what any frightened octopus would do...

Ssssssssplurt!

Oh dear!
Olive had sprayed a
cloud of black ink all
over the sea lions.
They did not
look happy.

"I thought you
were going to
eat me,"
said Olive.

Olive told the **sea lions** about the disappearing forest, and how she was trying to catch the **culprit**.

Hmmph!

"It can't be Bo, or Laynie or Sven, because none of them have **purple spines**," she said.

Olive felt bad about covering the sea lions in **black ink**. "Let me clean you up," she said. And she sprayed seawater all over them.

It turned into a **game!** The sea lions threw pebbles, shells and crabs to Olive, and she stopped each one with a **squirt** of water.

The **mystery** was solved!
A spiny purple sea urchin
had been **eating**
their forest.

Olive and the sea lions
soon found **more**
urchins. In some places
there were so many that
the kelp had **all gone**.

"Sea otters eat urchins,"
said Dale the dolphin.

"I know a family of otters
who need a new home,"
said Bo the bat ray.

So the animals asked
the sea otters to come and
live in their kelp forest.

And luckily the
sea otters agreed.

The **sea otters** ate some of the
sea urchins, and the **kelp forest**
began to grow again. Olive felt lucky
to live in such a beautiful place.

The
End